TWIBEING

PART 1: THE 100TH FAILURE

NEETU SUGANDH

Made with ♥ on the Notion Press Platform
www.notionpress.com

Contents

Prologue

"Her 100th failure will be her biggest success," Devnaksh raised his daughter Isha with this belief. He always knew she would fail each time she tried to achieve something, despite all her efforts. But he truly believed that there would be a time when she would recognise her powers. He has been waiting for that day. ON THAT DAY, he can disclose her true identity to her – she's a Twibeing.

Each time she failed and cried, he reassured her by saying, "Your 100th failure will be your biggest success." This belief kept her spirit high, and she developed a "never give up" type of attitude. She was determined to make her 100th failure – her biggest success, but she was not sure what form of success it will be.

CHAPTER ONE

Devnaksh's Worry

It was January 12, 2016, Isha's eighteenth birthday. She woke up in a jolly mood at 4 a.m. There was something special about the day; she could feel it. Never before did she feel like this on any of her birthdays.

All pepped up to participate in the martial arts competition to be held in her college, she left the house without waking up her father, Devnaksh.

Devnaksh woke up with a sombre expression and headed to Isha's room. She had left. He knew it was the day for her to face her 100th failure, but something made him anxious.

Devnaksh was a dusky, well-built, tall man with sharp features who was very protective of Isha. He had waited all these years for this day to arrive, but he was embarrassed at the same time.

"When Isha recognises her powers, I will have to disclose the past. Hope she doesn't hate me after that," he mumbled to himself. Then he closed his eyes and thought of Devisha, the woman he truly loved. "Devisha, the Twibeing will rescue you soon."

There was a time when Devnaksh could give up his life for Devisha. She was his strength, but time made her his weakness. The evil deception of the past made him lose her, and the only one who could rescue her was his daughter, Isha, who was a Twibeing.

He was bound by the rules of the Universe, so he had to wait for Isha to recognize her powers first before he disclosed the past to her.

She had always sensed that she was full of bad luck, but only Devnaksh knew the real reason behind her bad luck. He deliberately hid it from her.

He called her "determintelligent" – a strong blend of determined and intelligent, and that's what she truly was, even after all the bad luck.

CHAPTER TWO

THE VOICE OF THE HEART

As usual, the determinintelligent girl lost the martial arts competition at the last moment even though she gave her best. But somehow that moment for her was empowering; she heard an inner voice which seemed divine. "Your 100th failure will be your biggest success, Isha," she felt as if someone was trying to communicate with her through her heart. The feeling was unnatural.

She noticed a man, tall, fair, and plump with a long beard and almost her father's age, in the audience who smiled at her lovingly. The man had golden-brown hair till his shoulders and blue eyes which did not make him look Indian to Isha. He was the only one cheering for her, while the others were busy admiring the winner. She felt some sort of connection with him. Though her initial reaction was doubt because she had no one to love her except her father, Devnaksh, the feeling of doubt changed into sweetness automatically.

"Follow me," she heard the voice of the heart again. The man nodded slyly to confirm that it was him who was communicating with her through her heart. Then, he began to walk out of her college.

She followed him until he stopped in a lonely lane and looked back at her fondly.

Just when they were about to speak with each other, a squall of wind and screech of an eagle changed the man's expression into a frightening one.

"Run away from this place quickly," he communicated with Isha through the voice of the heart.

Isha found it strange, but she sensed great danger too. She started walking away from him without having a clue about the kind of danger that existed.

Suddenly, something on her left caught her attention. An extremely narrow path, releasing clear white mist, which could fit only one person at a time. It seemed as if the two big trees on her left moved away from each other to create a path. Surprisingly, no one else seemed to notice it, except her. She had crossed that place many times, but that path never existed before.

Through the voice of the heart, the man instructed her to enter the narrow path. She had no idea what was compelling her to listen to him, but there was a definite connection between him and her.

She began to walk towards the path. To her surprise, everything around her paused - the thunder squall and screech nullified, and there was complete silence. She could not quite believe all of it. She pinched herself to see if it was a dream, and “oops,” the pain made her realize “yes, it was REAL.”

Her shoes vanished as soon as she stepped onto that path. The positivity of the path made her move forward. She did look back to notice if things in the environment had gone back to normal, but the path’s entry had been covered by white clouds.

CHAPTER THREE

PAVITRANAGRI

Surrounded by white misty walls with an icy ground, the path had a small golden door on its right wall, at a distance of three hundred meters from where it began.

The door's height was four feet with a width of three feet, and it had no handle or lock. The door had a name engraved on it, "PAVITRANAGRI".

Isha thoroughly admired the beauty of the golden door until her attention was diverted by what existed on the opposite side of the path, right after the golden door. It was gloomy and full of dark fumes.

Isha heard a spooky whisper of a woman who invited her to walk into the gloomy side. But Isha was determinintelligent and well-trained by her father to recognize negative vibrations. She ignored the spooky whisper and waited to hear the voice of the heart.

"DON'T step into the dark side of the path," whispered the man she had seen earlier, through the voice of the heart. Isha quickly decided to enter the golden door that gave positive vibrations. What amused her was that it disappeared the moment she touched it and reappeared once she entered.

The door led her to a pure-white, misty place that was on a cloud. She slowly walked ahead and sensed a compassionate touch on her arm.

“Who is it?” she asked.

The white mist cleared a bit, and the soul of a woman became visible. She looked serene, walking in a white cotton saree draped in an unusual way down to her knees, teamed up with a white strapless blouse. The attire reminded Isha of a warrior – a simple warrior, maybe.

“Who could it be?” The eighteen-year-old Isha was stunned after taking a closer glance.

The woman had very similar facial features to Isha – beautiful, big eyes with a thick kohl liner on the lower lash line, slightly tanned skin, a small forehead, and a sharp nose. Her hair was long and silky down to her waist, just like Isha, and she looked just about four years older. She wore no jewellery or footwear, other than a thick gold string across her forehead.

“Happy Birthday, Isha! I am proud that you have been so brave; you are truly determinintelligent,” said the woman pleasantly.

Tears started rolling down Isha’s eyes, and extreme sadness took over her.

She asked the woman if she was her mother, as her father, Devnaksh, had described her mother to be beautiful and pure.

“Yes, indeed! I am your mother, Snehisha,” responded the woman kindly. “But the beautiful and pure woman that your father described to you is Devisha, the love of Saviour Devnaksh. You are named after her and destined to rescue her. Today I can disclose the secret to you because you could hear the voice of the heart after our long wait.”

Isha was quiet and listened intently to what her mother said.

Her mother disclosed that Devnaksh was not her father but the greatest savior in the Universe, Saviour Devnaksh, who protected her all this while. He, as well as the Heartians, was waiting for Isha to hear the “voice of the heart” before the past could be disclosed to her.

She revealed the long-awaited secret of why Isha was full of bad luck. “Your luck was snatched by Evoless, who has now captured the soul of your real father, Snehaksh.”

Snehisha needed Isha to inform Saviour Devnaksh about it soon.

Isha felt numb and emotional at the same time, but she immediately agreed to inform Devnaksh. “So, you and my father – are you alive?” she almost cried.

Her mother gave her a tight hug and asked her to stay strong as she was born to complete some great deeds.

She warned Isha that Evoless, her luck-snatcher, was planning to destroy Planet Earth and Heart.

The disclosure was a bit puzzling for Isha. "How can someone SNATCH luck?" she wondered. "And Planet Heart?" She had never heard of a planet like that before.

While she was beginning to inquire more, there was a sudden interruption. Isha and Snehisha heard the voice of the man who tried to communicate with Isha earlier. This time, Isha heard it loudly with her mother instead of hearing it through her heart.

"Snehisha, you need to rush back to Surakshanagri. Evoless's soldiers are looking for you," said the man.

"My child, I will have to rush back. But before I go, I must tell you that you are not a failure. Your 100th failure today is your biggest success," said Snehisha.

She reiterated that Isha must inform Saviour Devnaksh about Evoless capturing the soul of her father.

Isha did not want her mother to leave. But she saw her soul vanish.

"Go back to Saviour Devnaksh. We don't have much time," Isha heard the man through her heart.

"Who are you?" asked Isha loudly. She heard no response.

After a few seconds, she asked the same thing using her inner voice.

The man heard her and disclosed his name as Puraksh through the voice of the heart. He also revealed that he was a Heartian.

CHAPTER FOUR

The Narrow Path

"Paragonecto protecta," Isha heard a loud voice while standing alone in Pavitranagri. She sensed that there was someone outside the golden door. She walked cautiously towards it, gathered guts and touched it. Her touch made the door disappear and she saw Puraksh facing the gloomy side of the path without stepping into it. He was also barefoot, just like Isha after entering the thin lane.

He held a shiny, silver sword that cast a cloudy torrent, containing small souls of white dogs and doves. The cloudy torrent created a shield of protection at a distance of fifty metres from him.

His clothes had changed into that of a warrior, wearing a golden armour with white flowy pants. He also wore a gold string across his forehead.

The cloudy shield of protection was guarding him from someone who was roaring with anger on the gloomy side of the path. Isha stepped behind him with great difficulty due to the narrow width of the path. She was curious to see what was going on on the dark side of the path, but he was so tall and broad that she could barely see anything.

While maintaining his focus on the cloudy shield of protection, he again asked Isha to go back to Devnaksh, but she did not follow his instructions. Instead, she bent and tried to take a sneak peek into the dark side of the path. She saw a grim soul that appeared like a shadow, with no facial features, covered in a black cloth.

The grim soul was casting a torrent of black water at Puraksh through a weapon that was almost identical to Puraksh's sword; the only difference was that it was black. However, Puraksh's mystic shield of protection obstructed the torrent of black water.

Isha found Puraksh's sword purely fascinating. Its pure-white grip had a dog and a dove engraved on it, which was enchanting.

A little white dog from the shield of protection flew towards Isha, bowed his head, and tried to communicate with her through her heart. Isha understood what he said.

As per the little dog's instructions, Isha put her hand into his mouth and found a bone. She threw that bone powerfully from the little space she got from Puraksh's right, and it went flying into the evil soul's invisible mouth. His evil roar stopped immediately, and the torrent of black water disappeared. He was horrified to have experienced such a blow. He entered the smoggy wall on his left and disappeared.

There was a sudden silence. Isha smiled and winked at Puraksh while he looked at her with admiration.

By now, he had assessed her intelligence and powers and knew that she would not listen to instructions easily unless she was given answers.

“You are truly the TWIBIENG we have been waiting for,” he said, while requesting her to return to Saviour Devnaksh and disclose what had happened.

The term "TWIBIENG" left Isha flabbergasted.

Puraksh continued by saying the Heartians were waiting for their TWIBIENG and Saviour to return. He made another revelation that the narrow path was the path to Pavitranagri, which was a portal to Planet Heart.

Isha asked Puraksh why he wasn’t meeting Devnaksh directly. He informed her that he needed Devnaksh’s permission for that.

“It’s your 100th failure that made you hear the voice of the heart,” he said and reminded her to stay away from the dark side of the path as it was connected to the dark world.

Isha nodded and complimented Puraksh on his sword, saying it was mesmerizing.

"It’s a Paragonecto, Isha. All Heartians possess one for protection. Wait till you see Saviour Devnaksh’s Paragonecto," responded Puraksh as he departed.

Isha exited the path to Pavitranagri, while Puraksh entered Pavitranagri through the golden door to return to Planet Heart.

CHAPTER FIVE

Isha's Luck and Evoless

The moment Isha stepped out of the path to Pavitranagri, she saw herself standing outside the rusted gate of her house in Delhi Cantonment. She looked back but the path had disappeared. All she saw was the house of her neighbour across the road.

Isha took out her cell phone from her white bag, which showed the time as 6:30 a.m. She realized that the whole experience of meeting Puraksh and her mother had taken exactly 30 minutes. It was the first time things were happening so quickly in her life. Without wasting any time, she entered the veranda and rang the doorbell.

Devnaksh opened the door while pretending to be happy, though he was nervous internally. Isha immediately gauged he was faking it. She was used to his somber expression. But even with his somberness, he dearly loved her.

He was a teacher at a Govt. school where he taught children how to paint. Isha had expected him to be in his formal attire and neatly combed hair to go for his regular 8:00 a.m. to 3:00 p.m. job. However, things were different today. He was still in his night suit and had not showered yet.

"Happy Birthday," he said, hugging her tightly. "Why didn't you wake me up before leaving? I have cooked your favourite breakfast – mushty."

Isha smiled at the thought of eating mushty, but her priorities were different today.

She could sense that Devnaksh was waiting for her to tell him something. She also knew that he wasn't her father, but that had no impact on their beautiful and loving relationship.

"Yes, Dad, my 100th failure was my biggest success. I was able to hear the voice of the heart," said Isha exuberantly.

Devnaksh choked and immediately asked Isha to go inside the house. He peeped outside to see if anyone noticed them but found nothing strange, other than the usual activity of a few ladies gossiping with each other.

"How and when did it happen?" he asked intriguingly.

Isha disclosed that she heard the voice of the heart through which Puraksh guided her to enter the path to Pavitranagri, where she met Snehisha.

"You're a Saviour," she asked.

"Yes," he responded with a lot of embarrassment in his

voice.

"What exactly happened in the past?" Isha asked eagerly.

He was quiet for a few seconds, but then he decided to speak up.

"Too many things, Isha... way too many." He looked heartbroken thinking about the past.

It was the day he had waited for all these years when he could reveal Isha's true identity to her. Then what was making him so sad?

He disclosed that Isha was a TWIBIENG.

Isha immediately recalled Puraksh using that term as well.

"What's a TWIBIENG?" she asked curiously.

“A TWIBIENG is a being who has another half. When both the halves get together, they are so powerful that they can overcome any evil,” explained Devnaksh.

Isha was left dumbstruck.

Devnaksh continued that Isha's other half was a being whom no one had seen yet and her half would connect with her only when she eats the Luckruit, which was a “fruit of luck,” gifted to her by the Guiding Light.

Evoless had snatched the Luckruit when Isha was born because she wanted to ensure that the Twibeing never meets her other half and has no luck. The Luckruit turned into stone after Evoless killed Isha's parents.

Isha felt numb and began to inquire about Evoless and how the fruit turned into stone.

Devnaksh revealed that the true purpose of the existence of Isha's parents was to ensure that she eats the Luckruit, but when they were killed, it turned into stone. It can only turn into a fruit again when Isha touches it in the presence of her parents' souls.

Isha felt very sad and disclosed to Devnaksh that Evoless had captured her father's soul.

"That's not good news, Isha. Evoless wants you to hold the Luckruit in the presence of your parents' souls so that it could turn into a fruit again and she could eat it. She is definitely planning something destructive," Devnaksh revealed.

"Who exactly is Evoless?" asked Isha as that question was killing her from the inside.

"She is the shadow of an evil woman who keeps her identity concealed. In addition to killing your parents, she captured Devisha," disclosed Devnaksh.

Isha kept her hand on Devnaksh's shoulder empathetically. She was beginning to realise the reason behind his somberness.

He sadly confessed something that Isha wasn't expecting.

“I fell into Evoless’s trap of deception and made a terrible choice. The choice led to the death of your parents.”

CHAPTER SIX

Devnaksh's Confession

As soon as Devnaksh admitted his mistake of falling into Evoless's trap of deception, a ray of sparkling golden light surrounded him.

It was the "Guiding Light" that spoke, "Devnaksh, you have truly repented. I give back the 'power of ateetra' to you through which you will be able to show the TWIBIENG what had happened in the past. Once she sees the past, send her to Planet Heart."

Devnaksh nodded, after which the Guiding Light disappeared. He looked at Isha with an apologetic expression.

Isha loved him too much to believe that he could be responsible for anything bad. In fact, she was stunned to discover the copious hidden secrets of her life. She hugged him and pointed out that they must follow the instructions of the light.

Nodding his head in agreement, Devnaksh disclosed that he had sacrificed all of his powers in trying to find the secrets of the dark world. But now that he had got back the "power of Ateetra," he would be able to better prepare Isha to handle the dangers of the future.

Isha noticed the sadness on his face and changed his mood by asking if she could still call him father. This cheered him up instantly, and he admitted that he always considered her his daughter.

He highlighted that the Guiding Light had given them a second chance to defeat Evoless.

"The Guiding Light always watches us and helps in circumstances in which we need it the most, but it wants us to make the right choices," said Devnaksh.

The statement gave Isha some strength as she wondered if she could defeat anyone with the kind of luck she had.

"Isha, you are the only one who has the strength not to fall into Evoless's deceptions. Even with no luck, you can defeat her because you have the power of love. Your parents had the purest feeling of love out of which you were born. And the Heartians and I strongly love you. The strength of love cannot be beaten by anything evil," stated Devnaksh with a warning attached. He warned Isha that evil always tries to attack those who have love.

After listening intently to Devnaksh, Isha promised to defeat Evoless and said that she was determinintelligent for a reason and would make her 100th failure her biggest success.

Isha's promise elated Devnaksh, and he decided to show her the past through the power of Ateetra. He began to move the furniture to make some empty space in the centre of their small living room.

While helping him, Isha asked if he knew about Surakshanagri as that was the place where her mother went after she vanished from Pavitranagri.

Devnaksh revealed that Surakshanagri was a place where all pure souls were protected by the angels until they fulfilled their true purpose of existence. The Heartians and Saviours could see souls, and Isha was a heartian because of which she was able to see her mother's soul.

"The most loving angel of Surakshanagri, Angel Yashna, is your grandmother. Sadly, she died immediately after giving birth to your mother. The Guiding Light turned her into an angel," revealed Devnaksh.

Isha could relate to Devnaksh's somberness as it was painful to realize that all those whom she could have called family were no more.

"Mother told me I was destined to rescue Devisha," she stated.

Melancholy descended over Devnaksh on hearing Devisha's name. It was after a long time that someone had spoken about rescuing her. She had become a memory for him. She was his strength, but time made her his weakness.

Remorsefully, he sat on the floor which he had cleared to see the past. Isha sensed the extreme pain in his heart.

"My choices are the reason for Devisha's misery," unveiled Devnaksh.

Isha consoled him and inquired if he knew how to rescue her. He did not know the answer except for the fact that the TWIBIENG was destined to rescue her.

Isha did not probe further. Instead, she changed the topic by mentioning the Paragonecto and how much she admired it. Devnaksh told her she would be gifted one too in due course of time.

"Will I have a dog and dove engraved on the grip?" she asked.

"The Paragonecto is crafted by the Intelligent Tree of True Purpose. It has a connection with one's needs, true purpose of existence, destiny, or some aspect of one's life. It gets its powers from what's engraved on the grip," responded Devnaksh.

He added that Puraksh was gifted two pets by the Intelligent Tree of True Purpose – a dog and a dove, due to which he received a Paragonecto with a dog and a dove engraved on its grip, and that's why his Paragonecto released pure souls of dogs and doves.

Isha was intrigued to know about Devnaksh's Paragonecto as well as about the Intelligent Tree of True Purpose. He teased her by saying that she needed to focus on the past to know more.

“By the way, why did Puraksh feel the need to use his Paragonecto in the path to Pavitranagri?” asked Devnaksh curiously.

“He was fighting a grim soul in the dark side of the path,” confirmed Isha.

Devnaksh became serious again. “This means the path to the dark world has opened,” he said.

“What do you mean...was it *closed* earlier?” asked Isha.

"Yes," Devnaksh nodded with a serious expression.

CHAPTER SEVEN

THE TEN-YEAR OLD DEVNAKSH AND DEVISHA

Devnaksh and Isha sat opposite each other on the floor in the centre of their living room.

"So how exactly are we going to see the past?" Isha inquired.

Devnaksh explained that they would see the past through their closed eyes like it was a dream - that's how the power of ateetra worked. He warned Isha to keep her eyes closed until the dream was complete because while watching the dream of the past, they would be in no land and opening of the eyes would give strength to the evil to capture the person who opened their eyes and take them into the dark world.

Isha nodded in agreement. They closed their eyes, and Devnaksh made a request, "Our heart fancies the dream of the past."

With their closed eyes, they saw the first dream.

There was a ten-year-old boy and girl (Devnaksh and Devisha) in Pavitranagri, looking terrified. They were barefoot.

Angel Yashna appeared in her usual flared white silk gown and hugged them tightly.

She was carrying four Paragonectos in her hands - one had a cloud, the second had a big tree, the third had a river, and the fourth had a cave engraved on its grip.

Devnaksh and Devisha felt even more scared to see the Paragonectos because the Paragonectos belonged to their parents, and they had never seen their parents hand over the Paragonectos to anyone.

Angel Yashna disclosed sorrowful news that their parents had died and their souls had been taken to Surakshanagri. They were not supposed to die, but an evil woman from the dark world killed them.

"Who was the evil woman?" enquired Devnaksh furiously.

“No one knows. She was covered in a black cloth, and she was trying to open the Pureverse. That’s why your parents left you in Pavitranagri and fought with her on the path outside the golden door,” responded Yashna.

From their expressions, it seemed that little Devnaksh and Devisha didn’t quite understand what a Pureverse was.
“The Pureverse is a point after which ‘evil tries to reverse

anything that is good and pure.' It is the point where the golden door of Pavitranagri ends. After crossing it, one enters the dark world. Earlier, it was protected by the angels in the form of pure-white clouds."

Devnaksh and Devisha mentioned that they used to notice the Pureverse each time they entered the path to Pavitranagri with their parents. However, their parents never disclosed that the point was Pureverse, so the little children assumed it to be the end of the path, which was covered by white clouds.

Angel Yashna confirmed that from now on, the guardians of Parikshanagri will be protecting the Pureverse in the form of red clouds, and that will be the end of the path. The dark side would not be visible to anyone.

"Parikshanagri is a place where all blessed things are secured. No one knows where it is and no one has been there except for the Guiding Light. It has guardians who have never been seen by anyone in their true form. They appear as red clouds and talk to us. They are very powerful and will not allow the Pureverse to be opened again," she said.

Devnaksh's parents were the purest and bravest Saviours in the whole Universe. "How could any evil defeat them?" he inquired.

"The evil woman used some spells on the Pureverse which created dark fumes and made the angels vanish. Your parents fought her on the path to Pavitranagri, but she cast a torrent of some kind of evil black water, which killed them," said Yashna.

She also revealed that before fighting the evil woman, Devnaksh's mother put a curse that if the evil woman killed anyone, she would lose a finger. When the guardians of Parikshanagri arrived, they noticed four fingers on the floor in the narrow path to Pavitranagri. It was assumed that the evil woman lost four fingers after she killed the little children's parents.

It was painful for Yashna to disclose the horrifying news of their parents' death to the innocent children, but she had to abide by the order of the Guiding Light.

The children were kept away from the dark secrets of the Universe by their parents, but it was time to alert them.

She tried to cheer them up by mentioning that Pavitranagri, which had fascinated them since their childhood, would be their home now.

She touched the golden door of Pavitranagri, which disappeared with her touch and took the children into the narrow path to show them the red clouds on its right. She specifically asked them not to talk to the guardians because if their attention was diverted, the dark path would open.

Standing in a line in the narrow path, Devnaksh and Devisha looked at the red clouds with watery eyes. Then, Devisha turned to take a closer look at the name engraved on the golden door - PAVITRANAGRI.
"This door is called a Compasanor, Devisha. It only allows a person with a kind heart to enter. And this path to

Pavitranagri is only visible to those who are required to enter it. The Compasanor as well as the path checks the person's soul before allowing them to enter. You and Devnaksh will be safe in Pavitranagri," confirmed Yashna.

"What if that evil woman breaks in from the dark side of the path?" asked Devnaksh.

"Evil fears the guardians of Parikshanagri as they rip evil souls apart. The evil woman cannot defeat the guardians unless she has something that is uncommon, pure, and blessed," said Yashna.

Devnaksh asked if that thing could be a Paragonecto. Yashna explained that though Paragonectos were blessed, they were possessed by all saviors. There was no way of defeating the guardians using a Paragonecto.

After assuring the children that they were safe, she took them inside Pavitranagri and made them touch their parents' Paragonectos one last time, after which they disappeared.

"The Paragonectos have been sent to Parikshanagri. All blessed things are sent there after their purpose is completed," disclosed Yashna.

The children looked disheartened. Yashna sensed their excruciating pain, but there was no cure, except time.

Yashna warned the children to stay away from anything that looked like a black Paragonecto. She revealed that the evil woman who killed their parents possessed a black

Paragonecto through which she cast a torrent of black water. The guardians got a glimpse of the black Paragonecto before the evil woman disappeared. They informed Yashna that it did not have anything engraved on it, so they could not figure out the source of its powers.

The evil woman's deeds made Devnaksh furious, while Devisha was full of agony.

Yashna was upset too; she was very fond of their parents and visited them often in Veernagri, where all Saviours stayed. She knew the extreme pain of getting separated from loved ones because she had died immediately after giving birth to her daughter. She could only see her once in a while, when she visited the Earth.

She was worried about the two children and wanted them to live happily without troubles.

CHAPTER EIGHT

THE WALL OF WISHES

Yashna clapped her hands twice. Her clapping gesture produced a white rectangular cloudy wall in front of her.

"My lovelies, this is the 'Grand Wall of Wishes.' It will provide you with all the things you need, except those which are not good for you. The wall listens to you," said Yashna.

"I need a home for my lovelies," Yashna spoke to the Grand Wall of Wishes.

A golden door, which was a Compasanor, appeared in the centre of the grand wall. It had Devnaksh and Devisha's names engraved on it.

The children entered the door with Yashna and saw a living room with all the basic necessities. The walls, ground, and all other things had a cloudy texture and feel, just like Pavitranagri.

"Do you know what these clouds mean?" asked Yashna.

"They are the blessings of the angels. My parents told me when I visited Pavitranagri for the first time with them," responded Devisha.

"You are absolutely right, sweetheart. There are blessings everywhere in Pavitranagri. That's why our footwear disappears each time we enter the path of Pavitranagri; it's pure and blessed," confirmed Yashna.

She showed them some more interesting things present in their home. There was a white cloudy wall inside their living room, opposite to the Compasanor.

"It is the 'Mini Wall of Wishes' which is present in your home to help you with things you need inside your home," she stated.

"Kitchen," said Yashna, and a Compasanor with the name KITCHEN appeared on the Mini Wall of Wishes inside the house. They entered the kitchen and found a cooking stove, a gas cylinder, utensils, and a refrigerator.

"Devnaksh, why don't you open the refrigerator to see what all is in there?" suggested Yashna.

On opening the refrigerator, he found all the things of his choice – mangoes, apples, broccoli, mushrooms, tomatoes, milk, and some green chilies. Similar to the living room, the kitchen had white interiors with a cloudy texture.

Yashna pointed out that the Mini Wall of Wishes would give them their favourite food and would even cook for them.

The children seemed least interested in anything at that point. They missed their parents deeply.

They walked out of the kitchen, back into the living room. The Compasanor of the kitchen disappeared, and the Mini Wall of Wishes was empty again.

"Which room do you want to explore next?" asked Yashna.

"Study room," said Devisha out of respect for Yashna. Devnaksh didn't look too happy about it.

On hearing 'study room,' the Mini Wall of Wishes showed a Compasanor with the name STUDY ROOM. The study room had a bookshelf with many books along with a huge study table. There were two bags, two pencil boxes, and two lamps kept on the table. Its interiors were white too, with a cloudy texture.

The children recognised that the study material from their previous home had been brought into their new home in Pavitranagri.

CHAPTER NINE

Ms. Gyania

"Who is going to teach us now?" asked Devisha.

"Ms. Gyania, I request your presence in Pavitranagri," said Yashna.

"Appear anywhere, on time, I am here," they heard a loud, disciplined voice of a woman who appeared out of the pile of books lined up on the bookshelf.

"Hello Angel Yashna," said Ms. Gyania while walking towards her.

Dressed in a formal peach saree, Ms. Gyania wore a strange tiara with a golden book embedded on it, unlike Yashna's silver tiara with coloured stones.

"Hello Ms. Gyania, my two lovelies here would be your students from now," said Yashna while introducing the children to her.

"6 a.m. to 9 a.m., daily... Saturday and Sunday off. Does this schedule work for you?" Ms. Gyania asked the children.

They agreed.

“Very well then, we will start from tomorrow,” she said.

Yashna thanked Ms. Gyania, after which she disappeared back into the bookshelf.

“Ms. Gyania is the most learned woman in the Universe,” Yashna pointed out.

“That’s why there is a book embedded in her tiara,” whispered Devnaksh to Devisha.

Yashna informed them that Ms. Gyania had the power to teach ‘any subject to any being of any age anywhere at any time.’ The children seemed quite blank. Yashna could sense their misery.

"How did she manage to come out of the bookshelf?" enquired Devnaksh.

Yashna explained that Ms. Gyania was gifted with the power to travel through the book embedded on her tiara anywhere in the Universe, provided there was a book available at the destination.

Then, all of them walked out of the study room, back into the living room. The Mini Wall of Wishes inside their home was empty again.

Yashna explained that they could ask the Mini Wall of Wishes for any room they needed or anything they wanted inside their home.

"What about our houses in Veernagri, where we stayed earlier?" Devnaksh asked.

Yashna regretfully informed them that their houses would be acquired by other Saviours. It was the decision of the Guiding Light.

"The Guiding Light always watches us and helps in circumstances in which we need it the most, but it wants us to make the right choices," explained Yashna.

Devnaksh listened intently and requested Yashna to make the Grand Wall of Wishes invisible from the outside so that no evil could know that a house existed in Pavitranagri.

“The Grand Wall of Wishes is only visible to the owners of the home and the angels,” explained Yashna. The children, along with Yashna, then exited the home to be in Pavitranagri again.

Even after seeing the blessings in their new home, the children did not seem to be stable and looked extremely depressed.

Yashna could sense the children’s misery, but she was obliged to return to Surakshanagri, which is why she had to bid them goodbye and disappear.

The children requested the Grand Wall of Wishes to make the Compasanor visible to them so that they could enter their new home. The Grand Wall of Wishes, as well as the Compasanor, became invisible after the children entered their new home.

Pavitranagri was empty again in the eyes of others.

The first dream ended. Devnaksh asked Isha to open her eyes. It was 7:30 a.m. Isha noticed it took them thirty minutes to watch the first dream. Isha felt terrible for Devnaksh as the first dream made her realize that he had lost his family too at a very young age.

“You and Devisha looked adorable!” she tried to cheer him up. Devnaksh wasn’t too sure about himself, but he mentioned Devisha was adorable for sure.

Devnaksh and Isha got up and discussed a few things over breakfast while eating Isha’s favourite breakfast meal called mushty. It was a blend of mushrooms and onions sautéed together, served with toast and some tea. Isha shared her excitement about seeing her grandmother, Angel Yashna, and asked Devnaksh more about Veernagri, where he stayed until he was ten.

“It was a place in the mountains, covered with green vegetation, healing roses and wooden huts, where the Saviours stayed peacefully and happily. It was somewhere on Earth, no one knows where,” excitedly spoke Devnaksh.

"Healing roses meaning, did they heal people?" asked Isha.

"Yes indeed! Whenever we got hurt, all we had to do was touch the wound with the rose, and it would heal immediately. There were different colours to heal different types of wounds, but I guess there were none that could heal the wound of the black water due to which my parents died," he said.

Isha realised that Devnaksh could never get over the death of his parents. After a few seconds of silence, she enquired how they travelled from Veernagri to Pavitranagri.

“There was a stone wall in Veernagri. To enter Pavitranagri, we used to wait for the path to appear on that wall,” said Devnaksh. “The path automatically appeared when we were required to enter it.”

Isha also asked about Parikshanagri. Devnaksh mentioned that it was a place where all blessed things were secured. To acquire anything from there, one needed to pass eleven tests of purity laid by the guardians. He added that he had not visited Parikshanagri ever but had only heard of it from Yashna.

“Where was your Paragonecto? I did not see it in the dream,” Isha pointed out.

Devnaksh revealed that Saviours and Heartians received their Paragonectos at the age of sixteen, not before that.

"You and the other Heartians' children will only be able to receive Paragonectos once you defeat Evoless," stated Devnaksh.

The name “Evoless” agonised Isha, and she was getting more and more curious about Planet Heart and the Heartians. Devnaksh asked her to calm down. He explained that feelings of agony, anger, revenge, and impatience were not the cure for defeating Evoless because she survived off such feelings. Love, kindness, happiness, and patience were her biggest fears.

CHAPTER TEN

The Mirosee

At 8:30 a.m., Devnaksh made a call to the school in which he taught to inform them that he would be on sick leave for a few days. Isha had never seen Devnaksh miss work, not even for a single day. She was enjoying seeing the 'not so disciplined side' of him.

Devnaksh and Isha again sat down in the centre of their living room to experience the second dream. Devnaksh informed Isha that the dream might be long and asked her not to open her eyes until it ended. She agreed and closed her eyes.

Devnaksh made the request, "Our heart fancies the dream of the past."

With their eyes closed, they saw the second dream.

The ten-year-old Devnaksh was in his bedroom, looking deeply sad. He requested the Mini Wall of Wishes to bring him anything that had memories of his parents.

To his surprise, he received a 'mirosee' which his parents had left for him. It was an ancient, handheld mirror which the Saviours in Veernagri used to preserve their memories.

Devnaksh saw a memory when he looked into the mirosee. The memory was of a day before his parents' death when they gifted him a canvas along with a brand-new box of paint bottles and asked him to draw a whole new world on it.

Devnaksh loved to paint and spent almost the entire day painting the new world, while his parents admired him.

He was enjoying watching the memory when he heard a knock on the door. “Come in,” he said.

"Ms. Gyania will be here in an hour. Let's eat something; I'm hungry," said Devisha while walking into Devnaksh's room.

"Milk and cookies?" she asked the Mini Wall of Wishes. A big tray containing two glasses of milk and a bowl full of chocolate cookies appeared on the bedside table.

Devisha noticed the mirosee in Devnaksh's hands. “Did your parents leave you a memory in it?” she asked.

Devnaksh nodded and showed her the memory in which he painted a new world that his parents admired.

“I see that you put more colour on yourself than the canvas,” Devisha pointed out hilariously. Then she closely observed the world he painted.

It was violet and cloudy with a huge cave and a river right opposite to each other. Between the cave and the river, there was a wide path that led to the Intelligent Tree of True Purpose.

Devisha immediately recognised the Intelligent Tree of True Purpose from the description given by her parents – a big, blessed sparkling tree.

“Did you get the inspiration for the world from our parents' Paragonectos?” asked Devisha.

“Yes,” admitted Devnaksh. The Paragonectos fascinated him so much that when his parents asked him to draw a whole new world, he took inspiration from the shapes engraved on their Paragonectos.

“The idea of creating a cloudy world came from my father's Paragonecto, the river came from my mother's Paragonecto, the cave came from your mother's Paragonecto and the Intelligent Tree of True Purpose came from your father's Paragonecto,” revealed Devnaksh.

"Very original, I must admit," said Devisha in a teasing manner.

“The beautiful violet colour is my creativity,” he said in his defence.

Devisha laughed loudly and decided to get Ms. Gyania's feedback on his painting. They carried the mirosee with them to the study room.

CHAPTER ELEVEN

The Keyenter

"Appear anywhere, on time, I am here," said Ms. Gyania as she appeared out of the bookshelf, exactly at 6 a.m.

The children greeted Ms. Gyania; she felt sorry for what had happened with their parents.

Devnaksh showed Ms. Gyania his mirosee. She kept staring at it for a few seconds.

Devisha asked her how she found the painting.

"Oh my God! That canvas in the mirosee is a special canvas called 'the Keyenter' which means it is a key to enter a new world that is drawn on it," disclosed Ms. Gyania.

The children were astonished and inquired further about why Devnaksh's parents wanted him to create a new world.

Ms. Gyania explained that the creation of the new world could be the reason why the evil woman killed their parents, but she was not sure why they felt the need to create a new world.

"In the Universe, we create a new world only when something extremely evil is born or created so that the people of the new world can defeat it," she pointed out.

Ms. Gyania went into deep thought and checked if Devnaksh had the Keyenter with him.

He said he did not have it but could ask the Mini Wall of Wishes to get it from his previous home.

As soon as he asked for it, the Keyenter appeared on the study table. It was no longer a painting; the world had come to life on the canvas.

The children were extremely thrilled to see it.

Ms. Gyania observed it keenly. "The painting coming to life means that the world exists," she pointed out.

"What about people, animals, or birds? Since I did not draw them, does it mean the world will always be empty?" asked Devnaksh.

"I am not sure yet. This is the first time I am experiencing the creation of a new world on the Keyenter; until now I had only read about it. We will need to enter the world and ask the Intelligent Tree of True Purpose," said Ms. Gyania.

"What made you include the Intelligent Tree of True Purpose in this new world?" asked Ms. Gyania curiously.

Devnaksh revealed that his father had spoken about the Intelligent Tree of True Purpose many times. It was the tree which crafted Paragonectos, and Devnaksh was truly fascinated by it. It was also engraved on Devisha's father's Paragonecto. That's where he got the idea of including it in the new world.

"That was the reason you were chosen to draw the painting because your father knew that you would include the Intelligent Tree of True Purpose and the shapes engraved on their Paragonectos," said Ms. Gyania.

"How do we enter this world, Ms. Gyania?" asked Devnaksh.

She explained that they would need to place the painting at the point that their parents designated for the entry to the world. She guessed that the point was somewhere in Pavitranagri as the evil woman tried to attack them right outside it, and it was the place their parents visited right before they died.

"We must find the entry point to the new world soon, as many of the answers lie in it," she said.

All of them started walking out of the study room.

Devnaksh held the Keyenter. Ms. Gyania stopped and picked up a book from the table, which astonished the children.

"Well, I will leave this book inside the new world so that I can enter it whenever I want through the book," she said excitedly.

“Well, that’s great, Ms. Gyania,” said Devnaksh reluctantly, trying to hide his amusement for the book on her tiara.

"By the way, nice painting Devnaksh," said Ms. Gyania, smiling at him.

And they walked out of the home excited but clueless.

CHAPTER TWELVE

The Entry to Planet Heart

Ms. Gyania, Devnaksh, and Devisha began to stare at the cloudy wall of the round Pavitranagri and wondered where to start from.

"Time for some exercise, Devnaksh. You need to place the Keyenter at every point on the round wall of Pavitranagri," said Ms. Gyania. "The point that is designated for the entry will hold the Keyenter automatically."

Devnaksh looked a bit hassled as he had no idea how he would cover the whole wall.

Ms. Gyania smiled at his confused expression.

"Ms. Gyania, where should I begin?" he asked.

"Devnaksh, your 100th failure will be your biggest success. Try at least 100 times before you get tired," said Ms. Gyania. It was one of her smart ways of teaching.

Devisha felt empathetic and asked if she could help Devnaksh.

Ms. Gyania stated that only Devnaksh had the gift to discover the entry point to the new world, but she could be of some help, and the help was upon her to choose.

Devisha took a deep breath and decided to motivate him.

Devnaksh closed his eyes for a few seconds and then, he placed the Keyenter on the area of the wall behind them. Nothing happened. Devisha counted, "one," in a determined tone.

Next, he placed the Keyenter at the point next to it. Nothing happened. Devisha counted, "two."

Devnaksh's pace became faster as he continued, and Devisha's tone became more determined.

When he completed fifty tries, the cloudy texture of Pavitranagri turned golden, giving the place a glow, which meant that the angels were supporting the children in finding the entry point to the new world.

Ms. Gyania smiled at the sight. She was happy to see that the angels were in complete support of the creation of the new world and were getting fond of the two children. That's probably what she wanted as she had realised that Pavitranagri would be the portal to the new world once it opens.

The glow of the place became more and more golden as Devnaksh reached his 99th try. He reached the point on the wall that was opposite to the Compasanor – the golden entry door of Pavitranagri. It was time for the 100th try. Devnaksh was nervous.

"I know you will find it this time," assured Devisha. Her encouraging words gave him the strength to place the Keyenter exactly opposite to the Compasanor.

The angels glowed to the maximum; Devisha closed her eyes and began to pray.

"I couldn't do it, Ms. Gyania," she heard Devnaksh's voice and realised that he had failed.

On opening her eyes, she saw Devnaksh sitting on the ground with the painting beside him, feeling like a complete failure. She felt numb and said to herself, "I hope a miracle happens and Devnaksh succeeds."

Suddenly, the painting started to merge with the ground. Its size began to increase, and it turned into a full-fledged shiny violet door.

"Woo hoo," Devnaksh shouted with happiness. Devisha ran towards him and jumped with joy.

Ms. Gyania proudly told Devnaksh, "Your 100th failure was your biggest success, wasn't it?"

Devnaksh nodded his head in excitement.

They closely observed the violet door, which had no handle or lock, so they touched it and it opened, just like a Compasanor.

The three of them held hands and decided to enter the majestic door of the new world. However, they weren't sure if they had to jump through it or walk.

“Devnaksh, how would you have wanted to enter the new world?” asked Ms. Gyania.

"I would prefer simply stepping into it," responded Devnaksh after giving it a deep thought.

“Then, let's do so,” said Ms. Gyania, and all of them stepped through the door.

After stepping into it, they felt a cold ground under their feet, just like the ground of Pavitranagri, and there they were in the new world.

The three of them were in a state of euphoria. A violet ground and violet sky – it was nothing like they had ever seen before. The shiny violet entry door had disappeared from the top and was behind them.

“Welcome to Planet Heart – the sister planet of Earth,” they heard a loud, confident manly voice.

It was the Intelligent Tree of True Purpose that spoke.

Epilogue

Devnaksh made his 100th failure his biggest success. Will the Twibeing be able to do the same?

Will she defeat Evoless and get her luck back?

Will she rescue Devisha after finding out more about the past?

When will Puraksh return?

Will the Twibeing meet her other half anytime soon?

Why exactly did Devnaksh's parents feel the need to create a new world?

To find answers to these questions, wait for the next part of the Twibeing series.

www.ingramcontent.com/pod-product-compliance
Lightning Source LLC
LaVergne TN
LVHW040959150826
845672LV00002B/776

* 9 7 9 8 8 9 7 2 4 1 3 7 8 *